Help!
It's Harriet

Jean Ure

Illustrated by Stephen Lee

CollinsChildren'sBooks
An Imprint of HarperCollinsPublishers

First published in Great Britain by
CollinsAudio 1994
First published in Great Britain by
CollinsChildren'sBooks 1995

5 7 9 8 6 4

CollinsChildren'sBooks is a division of
HarperCollins*Publishers* Ltd,
77-85 Fulham Palace Road,
Hammersmith, London W6 8JB

Printed and bound in Great Britain
by HarperCollins Manufacturing Ltd, Glasgow

ISBN 0 00 675033 8

CONTENTS

HELP! IT'S HARRIET!

Harriet Johnson was a most unfortunate child. She could never do anything right. If she offered to help with the washing up, she would be sure to smash a glass or drop one of her mother's best dinner plates, while if you sent her down the road to buy a loaf of bread she would more than likely come back with three yellow dusters and a dishcloth because she had "seen a man selling them and felt sorry for him."

As for asking her to do a bit of vacuuming – well! Nobody who had had experience of Harriet's vacuuming would be foolish enough. Harriet was the sort of girl who only had to walk through a door for every ornament in the room to go crashing floorwards. Give her a vacuum and she broke everything in sight.

She was just as unfortunate at school. Nobody but Harriet could manage to lose the class register on the short journey between her classroom and Mrs Atkins' office. Only Harriet could bring the curtain down right on top of the baby Jesus in the middle of the Christmas nativity play. Harriet should never have been allowed anywhere near the curtain, of course, but that was when Mrs Middleton, her class teacher, had been new and hadn't realised what sort of child Harriet was.

Mrs Middleton had learnt, since then. She knew that whenever possible it was wise to keep Harriet out of things. The trouble was, Harriet was always so eager. When it came to Do A Good Turn Week she was especially eager.

Do a good turn week happened once a year, during the summer term. The top juniors were the only ones who were allowed to take part because they were the only ones considered responsible enough. Harriet was a top junior...

"So!" said Mrs Middleton, one morning at the beginning of June. (She tried not to look at Harriet as she spoke.) "I think we all know what Do A Good Turn Week means?"

Class 6 sat up straight on their chairs and did their best to look intelligent. Harriet sat up straighter and looked more intelligent than anyone. Harriet loved doing good turns.

"Who would like to tell us what it means?"

A forest of hands shot up, Harriet's in the lead. Mrs Middleton pretended not to see Harriet's.

"Alison?" she said. (Alison Leary was every teacher's favourite.)

"It means we get our-friends-and-families-to-sponsor-us-for-doing-a-good-turn-and-all-the-money-we-collect-goes-to-charity," gabbled Alison.

"Quite right, Alison! Thank you. And now I'm going to hand out the sponsor forms. One for Alison. One for Jonathan. One for Prahtiba…"

Mrs Middleton went round the class until she reached Harriet. When she reached Harriet, she came to a stop. Mrs Middleton was never quite sure about Harriet. The child meant well – at least, Mrs Middleton supposed that she did. It was just that everything she touched seemed to go catastrophically wrong. Mrs Middleton could still recall with a shudder the time she had locked Mr Marsh-Jones in the gardening shed. Mr Marsh-Jones was the head teacher. He had been in the gardening shed for over an hour, and might have been there all night if the school caretaker hadn't heard his cries for help.

"I thought he was a burglar," explained Harriet afterwards. "I was going to tell somebody, but then I went up the park and I forgot."

For one wild moment Mrs Middleton wondered if there was any way of persuading Harriet that it might be better if she didn't take part in Do A Good Turn Week; but then she looked at Harriet's face, all round and freckled and trusting, and she knew that there wasn't. With a sigh, she handed over the last sponsor form.

"And one for Harriet. Now please remember, everybody-" she placed a hand firmly on the back of Harriet's chair "-only offer to do tasks which you know you are capable of. We don't want any disasters, do we?"

Harriet shook her head. No! They didn't want any disasters.

"Just do your best," said Mrs Middleton. "And good luck!"

Harriet made a start that same afternoon. To begin with, she tried her mum.

"Sponsor you?" said her mum. "After last time?"

Last time Harriet had done her mum a good turn, which had been on her mum's birthday, she had left the garden hose running for almost four hours and washed away an entire flower bed.

"It's for charity," said Harriet.

"In that case I'd sooner sponsor you for *not* doing me a good turn."

"But that would be cheating!" said Harriet.

"I can't help that," said her mum. "There's no way I could survive having another good turn done for me. I'm sorry, Harriet, but there it is."

Harriet gave up on her mum and tried her sister instead.

"Sponsor *you*?" said her sister. "You must be joking! What am I supposed to sponsor you for? Ruining a pair of my best tights?"

"That was an accident," said Harriet. "You could sponsor me for cleaning up your bedroom."

"No way!"

"What about if I ironed some of your clothes for you?"

"I wouldn't let you within a thousand metres of my clothes! 'Specially not with an iron in your hand."

Harriet with an iron in her hand was lethal. The drawers were full of table cloths and handkerchiefs which bore the marks of Harriet's ironing.

"So, don't you want to sponsor me?" said Harriet.

"No," said her sister. "I do not!"

"I see," said Harriet.

It was really very puzzling. Her sister did nothing but moan and carry on about all the work she was expected to do – all the cleaning, all the tidying, all the homework. You'd think she'd be only too glad to let Harriet take some of it off her hands. People were extremely odd.

"Go and ask Dad." Her sister sniggered. "Ask him if *he'll* sponsor you!"

Harriet had a feeling that it might be better not to bother approaching her dad. Dad wasn't very pleased with Harriet just at the moment. He said that anyone who could try cleaning a car with paint stripper had to be congenital idiot. (Harriet had only been trying to help.)

"I think I'll ring Gran," she said.

"Don't you dare!" said Mum. "You leave Gran alone. We don't want you giving her a heart attack."

"I wouldn't!" said Harriet. "I just want to do her a good turn."

"Where's the difference?" said her mum.

It was very sad to be so misunderstood by one's own family.

Next day at school Alison Leary went round boasting that, "My sponsor form is practically filled up." Everyone had found *somebody* to sponsor them. Everyone except Harriet.

"Isn't it about time you got started?" sneered Alison.

Harriet wasn't too bothered; she was quite used to encountering these little setbacks. Her own family were peculiar: they didn't seem to want to be helped. But there was all the rest of the world to try! Harriet was not a girl to give up at the first refusal – or even at the twenty-first, if it came to that. "Keep at it!" was Harriet's motto.

On Saturday morning Harriet did the rounds of the neighbours. Some of them were lucky enough to be out. Others, not so lucky, opened the door before they realised who it was.

She caught Mrs Mason taking in the milk bottles. At the sight of Harriet, Mrs Mason grabbed the milk and made a dash for the front door. She wasn't quite quick enough.

"Would you like to sponsor me for doing you a good turn?" said Harriet.

Mrs Mason turned pale.

"Oh, no, Harriet!" she said. "Please!"

Harriet had done Mrs Mason a good turn last year, when Mrs Mason had been ill with flu. She had trimmed her front hedge into an interesting shape. Well, Harriet had thought it was an interesting shape. Mrs Mason had never got over it. (Neither had the hedge.)

"I really don't think," said Mrs Mason, faintly, "that I could stand it. I'm sorry, Harriet. You'll have to try somebody else."

Harriet marched on up the road. The man from Number 10 was walking his dog. He took to his heels and ran when he saw Harriet.

Unperturbed, Harriet stomped up the path of Number 12 and hammered with the knocker. (Harriet did everything loudly.)

Mum's friend, Mrs Barnes, opened the door.

"Hallo, Mrs Barnes," said Harriet. "I wonder if you'd like t…"

"No!" Mrs Barnes almost screamed it in her panic. "Whatever it is, the answer is no!"

"But I only w…"

"I can't stop," said Mrs Barnes. "I'm polishing the guinea pig… I mean I'm bathing the car… I mean I'm – I'm busy!"

The door shut in Harriet's face. Philosophically, grown-ups were often rather unbalanced, in Harriet's experience. Harriet clambered over the low wall that divided Number 12 from Number 14. The lady at Number 14 must have been watching, for a curtain twitched as Harriet approached, and from somewhere inside the house a terrified voice cried, "Help! It's Harriet!"

The message spread rapidly – "Harriet is coming! Harriet is coming!"

At Number 16 she heard the sound of doors slamming.

At Number 18 a small boy shouted at her through the letter box: "We're out!"

Everybody knew Harriet too well.

And then she reached the house on the corner.

A new lady had come to live in the house on the corner. A lady called Miss Fanshawe. A lady who had never heard of Harriet ...

"Yes?" said Miss Fanshawe.

Harriet and Miss Fanshawe stood looking at each other. Miss Fanshawe was a tall, thin person wearing a dress of spinach green: Harriet was a short, dumpy person wearing blue dungarees. Miss Fanshawe's hair was like a badly made bird's nest: Harriet's was like a dish mop. Miss Fanshawe had an air of being deeply flustered: Harriet was business-like.

"Would you like to sponsor me for doing you a good turn?" said Harriet.

Miss Fanshawe emitted a little breathless squeak.

"I should *love* to sponsor you for doing me a good turn!" She clasped her hands together as if in prayer. Harriet blinked.

"One should always trust in the Lord," said Miss Fanshawe. "He never fails one."

"It's for charity," said Harriet.

"Yes, yes! Indeed so! The church fete, this very day. I am in desperate need of a helper! I have just heard that my mother has been taken poorly and I must go to her.

"But what," cried Miss Fanshawe, "am I to do about my bran tub? I gave the Vicar my word that I would be there! Do you think, little girl, that you would be capable of taking care of a bran tub?"

"Yes," said Harriet. She didn't know what a bran tub was, but Harriet never let little things like that stop her.

She would have said yes if she had been asked to take care of a herd of wild rhinos. There was almost nothing that Harriet didn't believe herself capable of.

"Such a relief!" said Miss Fanshawe. "You have made me so happy! I will help you and you will help me. What could be better?"

Miss Fanshawe beamed down upon Harriet. Harriet held out her sponsor form.

"Shall we say five pounds?" said Miss Fanshawe. "For the day?"

"That sounds all right," said Harriet. (She bet it was more than Alison Leary had got.)

"Then let us go right away! It's only up the road, in the church field. There will be just enough time for me to explain things to you on the way."

Miss Fanshawe explained quickly but carefully. A bran tub, it seemed, was just another name for a lucky dip.

"Always very popular. The children simply put their hands in and pick something out. This is the bran tub, here ..." (full of what looked like sawdust and exciting little packages) "... and there, in the tent, is the back-up." (The back-up was a big plastic dustbin sack full of more exciting little packages.)

"When you feel the tub is getting empty, just go and help yourself from the sack. It's 25p a go, and whatever you do don't let them churn things about and spill the bran. It makes a nasty mess on the grass," said Miss Fanshawe. "You will have to be stern with them. They are to take the first thing that comes to hand."

"I'll be stern," said Harriet.

"Don't forget," said Miss Fanshawe, "the extra presents are in the sack.

Miss Fanshawe went off to her mother: Harriet took up her position behind the bran tub.

"Lucky Dip!" bawled Harriet. "25p a go!"

The lucky dip was every bit as popular as Miss Fanshawe had said, in spite of some of the bigger boys complaining when they picked girls' things.

(The girls didn't seem to mind picking boys' things.)

One child tried to claim a free go, "Cos I picked this book and I've already read it," but Harriet was standing no nonsense.

She took her duties as guardian of the bran tub very seriously.

"You can just go away and read it again," she said.

"Shan't!" said the child. "You can have it back!"

"Yeah, and you can have this doll back an' all!" yelled a little boy.

"And this bag!" cried another. "Bags is girls' things!"

Suddenly, it seemed that Harriet had a rebellion on her hands. She decided to go and get some more presents. Perhaps the next lot would be a bit better.

Harriet ran into the tent, tore open the nearest black sack, seized an armful of prettily wrapped parcels and ran back with them to the bran tub, where a long queue had already formed.

The second lot of presents, although rather eccentric, went down better than the first. Harriet watched as small hands ripped open packages and pulled out the contents. There were hair nets, sponge bags, bed jackets, teacosies, bath caps, paper knives, bed socks, bubble baths, bath cubes, magnifying glasses, paper handkerchiefs... If the parents seemed slightly puzzled, at least the children were

happy. Harriet had no more complaints.

By the end of the afternoon, both the bran tub and the black plastic sack were empty. The field, meanwhile, was full of joyous small children having battles with bath cubes, using hair nets as catapults, shredding paper handkerchiefs into confetti, enlarging startled insects with magnifying glasses, conducting mock sword fights with paper knives, squirting each other with scent sprays...

Some of them were wearing tea cosies on their heads, some had bed jackets tied round their shoulders like capes. All were wildly happy. Never had a bran tub been such a success!

By the time Miss Fanshawe came hurrying back, the field had mostly cleared. The bath cube battles had ceased, the tea-cosied warriors been carted off home. Flushed with the sense of a task well done, Harriet handed over the money pot.

"Oh, that's very good!" said Miss Fanshawe. "That is excellent! The Vicar will be delighted! I wonder, little girl, now that you've done such a magnificent job with the bran tub, whether you would care to do something else for me?"

"Would I get another five pounds?" said Harriet. After all, it was for charity.

"You drive a hard bargain," said Miss Fanshawe, "but I'm desperate. Yes, all right, another five pounds! It's very simple. All I want you to do is take the other sack..."

"What other sack?" said Harriet.

"The other sack in the tent – the one marked 'Old People'. Just take it across to the big marquee and hand out the presents to my old ladies and gentlemen. I have to go and pick up some medicine for my mother, but I shall be back before you've finished. Do you think you could manage that?"

"Yes," said Harriet. She could manage anything.

Miss Fanshawe went off to fetch her mother's medicine leaving Harriet in charge of the Old People's sack. Harriet's heart swelled with pride. Supervisor of the presents! She bet Alison Leary hadn't been trusted with anything half as responsible.

Taking her second sack by the scruff of its neck, Harriet marched off across the field to the big marquee. Inside there were lots of old people sitting on chairs, awaiting the moment when they would be given their presents. Harriet heard one old man mutter, "I hope it's better than last year. Bloomin' awful they were, last year."

"These are really *good* presents," said Harriet.

"How do you know?" said the old man.

"They feel good," said Harriet.

"Well, get on with it, then!" shouted an old lady. "Don't finger 'em – dish 'em out!"

Self-importantly, dragging the sack behind her, Harriet began to walk round the old people handing out the presents. She was a bit shaken when the old lady who had shouted at her tore the wrapping paper off a water pistol, and the old man who had grumbled about last year unwrapped a toy motor car, but they were Miss Fanshawe's presents, not hers. Miss Fanshawe, presumably, had chosen them. Harriet was only giving them out.

Doggedly, Harriet continued. Another old man unwrapped a bag of marbles. An old lady unwrapped a teddy bear. Some grown-up helpers, standing by the tea urns, began to mutter.

"Most unsuitable!"

"Look at that! What is it?"

"My dear, it looks like a yoyo!"

Harriet began to feel a trifle uneasy. She reminded herself once again that it was Miss Fanshawe who had chosen the presents, not her.

"A skipping rope! This really is too much!"

"I've a good mind to complain to the vicar."

The unwrapping went on. An old man unwrapped a wriggly snake. An old lady unwrapped a baby doll. It certainly did seem a bit odd.

A strange and troubling thought occurred

to Harriet. She glanced down at the sack she was holding. There was a big white label attached to it. On the label, in big black letters, were quite plainly printed the words, BRAN TUB ...

Oh, dear... thought Harriet. ...I seem to have made a slight mistake.

All the children were at home playing with the old people's presents, and all the old people were playing with the bran tub presents! All over the marquee were old folk throwing fivestones, rolling marbles, flipping tiddly winks, blowing up balloons, blowing party hooters, crashing their toy motor cars, filling their water pistols from the tea urns – they were having a wonderful time!

Miss Fanshawe arrived just as the old man with the wriggly snake was chasing an old lady across the marquee. The old lady was giggling and giving little screeches.

Miss Fanshawe smiled, uncertainly, and began to make her way across to Harriet.

"Here I am," she said. "I promised I wouldn't be long. I'll give you your..."

Her voice trailed away. An old man making train noises had just gone chugging past her.

Nearby, an old lady was sprightly jumping in and out of a skipping rope being turned by two of her friends. One of the friends was chewing bubble gum. Even as Harriet and Miss Fanshawe watched, she blew it out of her mouth into a large pink blister.

"What," whispered Miss Fanshawe, "is going on?"

"They're playing with their presents," said Harriet.

One of the helpers came over.

"It's a disgrace," said the helper. "I shall complain to the Vicar!"

The Vicar had just appeared in the entrance to the marquee. He was walking towards them, trying his best to keep his eyebrows in place. It didn't do for a vicar to show signs of alarm.

"You wretched child!" shrieked Miss Fanshawe. "You've mixed up the sacks!"

Even as she spoke, a surge of excited old people were ambushing the Vicar.

"Lovely party!" they chorused. "Wonderful presents!"

"Darn sight better than last year," said the old man who had complained.

"You can say that again," agreed the old lady who had shouted at Harriet to get on with it. She pointed her water pistol full of cold tea at the Vicar. "Better than bloomin' bed jackets!"

The Vicar, bravely wiping cold tea off his face, came over to Harriet and Miss Fanshawe.

"Well, I must congratulate you, Miss Fanshawe! You've done a simply splendid job with the old folk. I've never seen them so..." he paused as the old man with the wriggly snake rushed past him "... so lively!"

Miss Fanshawe gave a rather sickly smile as she handed Harriet her ten pounds.

"I enjoyed that," said Harriet. "I'll come and help you again next year, shall I?"

"Thank you, little girl." Miss Fanshawe brushed a trembling hand across her forehead. "That would be lovely."

As Harriet left the marquee she heard Miss Fanshawe whisper rather urgently to the vicar.

"What is the name of that child? Do you know her?"

"Oh yes!" said the Vicar. "That's Harriet. Everyone knows Harriet!"

Harriet beamed. She supposed she *was* rather well known!

A VERY BUSY SORT OF DAY

"Oh, Harriet, really!" Harriet's mum stared in exasperation at the trail of muddy bootprints leading across the kitchen floor and out into the hall. "How many times have I told you to take your boots off at the back door?"

About a hundred times, probably. So many times that Harriet had lost count. It was a funny thing about Harriet's boots: once they were on her feet they seemed to become permanently attached to her. She always meant to take them off; but then she would come rushing in, all busy and excited, to fetch a ball or find something to eat, and before she knew it there would be great gollops of mud all over the place and Mum would be going demented.

"It really is too bad!" said Mum. "Today of all days!"

Harriet hung her head. Today was Good

Friday and Gran was coming to stay. She was arriving at four o'clock, in time for tea.

"What is the point," said Mum, "of my bothering to wash the kitchen floor if you're just going to march in and trample over it?"

"I'll clean it up," said Harriet.

"Well, go on, then! And just watch what you're doing. We don't want any more accidents like the time you left the bathroom tap running."

When Harriet had left the bathroom tap running, all the water had come flooding along the top landing and cascading into the hall.

"I'm going upstairs to make Gran's bed," said Mum. "By the time I come down I want to see that floor spotless."

Harriet quite enjoyed cleaning the kitchen floor. She filled a bucket at the sink and squeezed in some washing-up liquid. She wasn't sure how much to use so she went on squeezing until all the bubbles came frothing up over the side. The bucket was rather heavy and as a result quite a lot of water, in fact most of the water, went slopping on to the floor. But that was all right because, after all, that was where it was meant to go. (Some went slopping over Harriet as well, but you expected to get a bit wet when you were cleaning floors.)

Next she took a nice new sponge, a bright pink one, from under the sink, and started mopping. Mop mop mop, went Harriet, with her bright pink sponge. The water sploshed and splattered and went spreading in circles across the kitchen. Harriet came to the conclusion that perhaps there *was* a bit too much of it.

Mopping at it with a sponge was like trying to empty a swimming bath with a tea cup. She needed something bigger than a sponge, she needed – a towel!

Harriet tore the towel off the back of the door, spread it over the floor and trampled on it. Then she tore the tea towels off the rack and spread them on the floor and trampled on them, as well. That was better! Now she was getting somewhere.

Another towel – another *two* towels – a bit of kitchen roll – *lots* of kitchen roll – *all* the kitchen roll – and there! The floor was cleaner than she had ever seen it. A bit damp, perhaps, but it would soon dry up. Mum would be pleased.

Harriet stood up. She took a step backwards, the better to admire her handiwork. Crash! went Harriet, straight into her bucket.

All the soapy water that hadn't escaped the first time went flooding out across her clean floor.

"*Bother*," said Harriet.

Now she would have to start all over again. She took the last four towels from the drawer and laid them out and trampled on them. She took all the tea towels and a new kitchen roll.

The cat appeared through the cat flap and sat for a moment, watching. The minute Harriet had finished and the floor was merely damp once again instead of sopping wet, it trod slowly and deliberately right across the middle, leaving a trail rather like Harriet's boots had done.

Harriet ran at it with a yell. The cat, whose name was Fat Cat, casually leapt on top of the refrigerator and began washing himself.

"*Honestly,*" said Harriet. "What is the point of my bothering to clean the kitchen floor if you just come in and walk all over it?"

There weren't any more towels left, nor any more tea towels. Harriet mopped up the pawprints with kitchen roll. Then she took the empty bucket back to the sink and filled it with all the dirty wet towels and tea towels. That was a job well done! No one could say she hadn't made her contribution to Gran's visit.

Harriet wiped her hands on the back of her

jeans and went upstairs to find Mum.

"I've done the kitchen floor for you," she said. "I've done it better than you do. I've done it properly."

"Good" said her mum. "I'm glad to hear it."

Mum went back downstairs. Seconds later there was an outraged shriek.

"Harriet, for goodness sake! What on earth have you been up to?"

Harriet peered over the banisters.

"Washing the floor," she said.

"Washing it? It's like a skating rink!"

"It'll dry," said Harriet.

"Not before someone's broken their neck – and what have you done with all my towels? Oh, Harriet, *really!*"

"Wasn't my fault," said Harriet, jumping down the stairs in two big jumps and crash-landing in the hall. "The water was too wet!"

"Too wet!" That was her elder sister, Lynn, standing jeering in the kitchen doorway. "You mean, you used too much of it!"

"No, I don't. I mean it was too wet!"

"So what do you expect water to be? *Dry?*"

Harriet opened her mouth, but Mum got in before her.

"Just be quiet, the pair of you." Mum was stuffing wet towels and tea towels into the washing machine. "Go away and get out from under my feet! I have things to do."

Lynn sniffed, and vanished. Harriet stayed where she was.

"Would you like me to help you?" she said.

"Not really," said Mum. She had had experience of Harriet's helping. "I'd rather you went and shut yourself in a cupboard for a few hours."

Harriet thought about it.

"There isn't a cupboard big enough," she said.

"More's the pity," said Mum.

"Anyway, I want to help you get things ready for Gran. I like helping you," said Harriet.

Mum groaned.

"What shall we do first? Shall we make something?"

"I shall make something," said Mum. "I shall make crab patties." Crab patties were Gran's favourite. She always had crab patties - lovely little pastry pies with crab meat inside. "You can stand and watch."

"I don't want to stand and watch! I want to help you. I'll get all the things out that you need and hand them over to you like in an operating theatre... You can be the surgeon," said Harriet, "and I'll be the head nurse. We'll spread them all out on here – " Bossily she indicated the kitchen table, " – and when you want something, you just say."

Harriet's dad looked in at the kitchen door.

"Need any help?" he said. "Ah no! I see you've got Harriet!"

Harriet's dad chuckled and went away again. Harriet's mum smiled, weakly.

"Are you sure," she said to Harriet, "that you wouldn't rather go and do something in the garden?"

"No," said Harriet, "'cause then I'd get my feet muddy. I'm going to stay here and hand you things."

In the process of handing things Harriet dropped the tin of crab, broke a plate, skidded on the damp floor and crashed into Mum so that Mum cut herself with a knife and had to go away and put a plaster on her finger, knocked a glass dish off the table and tried to pass the sugar sifter instead of the salt. Apart from that, she was quite helpful.

"I reckon it's a lot easier with two people, don't you?" said Harriet.

"I don't know about easier," said Mum. "It's certainly more eventful."

Harriet watched proudly as Mum put the finishing touch to the patties. How splendid they looked! She and Mum had done a good job. Gran would enjoy her patties.

On top of the refrigerator, in a big heap, sat Fat Cat, resting on his elbows. He didn't make a sound but his eyes slid sideways, from the empty crab tin on the draining board to the lovely plump crab patties in their dish. Fat Cat enjoyed crab patties even more than Gran did.

"There!" said Mum. "We'll pop them in the oven and by the time we've finished the washing up and laid the table they'll be done."

Harriet did the washing up; she liked washing up. She liked making soap bubbles and blowing them round the sink. Dad popped his head round the kitchen door while she was doing it and said, "Need any help? Want me to wipe?" And then,

remembering "Oh, no, I can't! We haven't got any tea towels. Jolly good!"

Men were pretty useless, thought Harriet. She looked in the drawer where Mum kept the clean rags. An old T-shirt; that would do.

She broke another couple of plates while she was wiping up but it wasn't her fault. It was the washing up liquid. There was something wrong with it; it made things too slippy.

Mum came back and they took the crab patties out of the oven. The smell was delicious! It wafted enticingly up to the top of the refrigerator. Fat Cat twitched his whiskers and wiggled his paws in anticipation. Gran was a soft touch – and he was her favourite cat. He knew how to get round her.

Fat Cat sat there, laying his plans. First he would rub round Gran's ankles, butting at her with his head and weaving in and out. Then he would arch his back and go up on his tippity toes, with his tail in the air. Then he would let out a piteous yowl, indicating that they starved him in this place. Finally, he would stand with his front paws on Gran's knees, gazing at her with all the love and devotion that he was capable of. And after she had shared her crab patties with him he would go to sleep on her nice soft lap. That is, if he couldn't work out some way of getting to the patties first...

Mum was in the middle of laying out the patties on a wire tray when Lynn came into the kitchen and said, "Auntie Margaret's on the phone."

"Oh, all right," said Mum. She turned to Harriet. "Do you think you could put the rest of the patties on this tray and then put the tray in the cupboard for me? Could you manage to do that, do you think?"

"Of course I could," said Harriet. What did Mum take her for? A 6-year-old?

"Just be careful," said Mum, "and don't drop any."

Harriet couldn't understand why it was that people had so little faith in her. Carefully, she laid out the rest of the patties and took the wire tray across to the cupboard. On her way to the cupboard she tripped over one of her feet. (Harriet was always tripping over her feet. They didn't seem to be the same as other people's.) As a result, the tray went shooting out of her hands and across the room.

It was a good thing the floor was so clean, thought Harriet, crawling round on her hands and knees gathering up crab patties. None of them had broken, though one was a bit battered at the edges, as if mice had got to it. She wondered whether to eat it or let Mum think that there were mice in the cupboards. She was still wondering when from the corner of her eye she saw something go flying past the kitchen window. A football!

Harriet dumped the patties in the cupboard, tore across the kitchen, wrenched open the door and went galloping out, hollering and hallooing, into the garden. She was just in time to catch her great enemy, George Pink, hauling himself over the fence.

"Hey, you, Pudding Face!" screeched Harriet. "Get out of our garden!"

"Want my ball back," said Pudding Face.

"*Please*," said Harriet.

"*Please*," said Pudding Face.

"What's it doing here, anyway?"

"Kicked it, didn't I?"

"What for? Cos you can't aim straight, I suppose."

"Wind took it."

"Isn't any wind."

"Is in our garden."

"Must all be coming from you, then!"

Harriet chortled happily at her own wit. She and Pudding Face routinely exchanged insults.

"Can I have my ball back now?" said Pudding Face.

"You've forgotten that little word," said Harriet.

"I already said it!"

"Say it again."

"Shan't!"

"Won't get it back, then."

Harriet squidged across the wet lawn, scuffled under a dripping redcurrant bush and emerged triumphant with a muddy football clutched to her chest. Carelessly, she tossed it in the air.

"Want it?"

"Give it us!"

"Tut, tut! *Manners*," said Harriet.

With slow deliberation, Harriet dribbled the ball across the squelching lawn.

"PLEASE!" bellowed Pudding Face.

"Just don't do it again," said Harriet, tossing the ball over the fence, "or I'll set my cat on you."

"Yah! Your cat's a poof cat!" yelled Pudding Face, from the safety of his own garden.

Harriet took a running jump at the fence.

"Button it, squitter bonce!"

"Prune features!"

"Rabbit teeth!"

"Scum bag!"

Satisfied that the full ritual had been observed, Pudding Face trundled off with his football. Harriet returned indoors. Had she been wearing her boots she would naturally have remembered to take them off; as she wasn't, she marched blissfully across the kitchen floor in muddy slippers, leaving the usual trail behind her.

Two minutes later, her dad opened the kitchen door, took one look and hastily closed it again.

Two minutes after that, Harriet's mum opened the kitchen door.

"HARRIET!" she bawled. "You come down here this instant!"

By the time Harriet had wiped the kitchen floor, *again* (under strict supervision, this time using a cloth from the bathroom) it was almost four o'clock. Gran was due at any minute.

"Now that you're here you can take some of the food in," said Mum. "We'll have it all nice and ready, so that Gran can sit straight down."

Mum turned to open the cupboard door. As she did so, an enormous great fat cat came walking out. It was twice the size of any normal cat. It had a big fat beam on its face.

It smelt of crab patties...

Mum screamed. "Oh, no!"

The wire tray was completely empty. "Oh, I can't bear it!"

"I put them in the cupboard," said Harriet, "like you said."

"Yes, and you put that cat in the cupboard with them!"

"I never," said Harriet.

"In that case, you didn't bother to close the door properly! Oh, Harriet, really! Can't you do *anything* right?"

"Wasn't my fault," said Harriet. "It was that Pudding Face."

"What are you talking about? He isn't even here... And don't call him Pudding Face!"

"Why not?" said Harriet. "He calls me Scum Bag."

"Don't make excuses! Of course it was your fault! You can't be trusted with the simplest task – I've a good mind to stop your pocket money. In fact, I *shall* stop your pocket money! I shall tell your dad not to give you any. You don't deserve it, you're nothing but a menace – and oh, heavens, there's the front door bell! That'll be Gran! *Now* what are we to give her for tea?"

While Mum and Dad and Lynn gathered in the hall to greet Gran, Harriet skulked in the kitchen with Fat Cat (now back on top of the refrigerator, washing himself). How mean of Mum to stop her pocket money! She had only been trying to help. Grown-ups didn't deserve being helped if this was the way they thanked you.

The kitchen door opened and Lynn poked her head round.

"Oh, there you are," said Lynn. "You're in disgrace. You're not going to get any pocket money."

"Think I care?" said Harriet. "It's vulgar to care about money."

"Oh, yes?" said Lynn, and she smiled one of her superior smiles. "Mum says you're to go in and say hallo to Gran."

As Harriet sidled into the sitting room she heard Mum say, "... a slight accident, I fear. Someone who shall be nameless forgot to shut the cupboard door. So now all we can offer you is sandwiches of some kind or another."

"Sandwiches," said Gran, holding out her arms to Harriet, "would be delightful! In fact what would be most delightful of all would be plain bread and butter. I was in two minds whether to ring you before I came and say whatever you do, don't make crab patties. But then I thought perhaps you may already have done so."

"Don't you like crab patties any more?" said Harriet.

"My dear, I shall never eat another crab patty as long as I live! I ate some the other day and they must have been off. Decidedly off. They made me very sick and bad. My stomach is still unsettled. So whoever it was who left the cupboard door open, I am really quite grateful to them."

Harriet turned, slowly, to look at her mum. Her mum looked at her dad.

"How awful if Gran had had to eat crab patties," said Harriet.

Dad sighed and slipped his hand into his pocket.

"And where is my favourite cat?" said Gran. "Why hasn't he come to see me?"

Gran's favourite cat was curled up in a tea cosy on top of the refrigerator, too fat to move and dreaming of crab.

"It's not that he doesn't love you," said Harriet, anxiously, "it's just that he's had a very busy sort of day."

"Haven't we all?" said Harriet's mum.

THE PEASANTS' REVOLT

"That child there!" said Miss Beadle. "What is your name?"

Heads turned to see whom she was talking to. Harriet's turned with them.

"You!" said Miss Beadle.

"Me?" said Harriet.

"Yes, you! At the back! What is your name?"

"Harriet Johnson," said Harriet.

"Then I shall not tell you again, Harriet Johnson. Sit straight upon your chair and do not fidget. I cannot teach a history lesson if I have pupils who are constantly a-twitch. It shows a lack of attention."

Harriet was hurt. She had been attending! They were learning about the peasants' revolt; how all the peasants, in 1381, had "gathered themselves in great routs" and gone marching off to London, under Wat Tyler, to see Richard II and demand that he right their wrongs.

Harriet, in her imagination, had been Wat Tyler himself, boldly stepping out at their head, waving his banner to encourage the faint-hearted. It was true that in her enthusiasm she might have clattered her feet a bit, and bounced her pencil case on to the floor, and banged her chair into Alison Leary at the next table, but that wasn't because she had not been attending. It was because she *had* been attending.

Harriet was, as a matter of fact, deeply interested in the peasants and their wrongs. It seemed to her that some of the things they complained of were not so very different from the things that she herself complained of – being forced, for instance, to come to school every day whether you felt like it or not.

Being forced to sit at a table doing maths cards or spelling when you would far rather be running about outside kicking a ball. Being forced to eat yuck in the school canteen when what you would really have liked was a bag of chips or a bar of chocolate.

Children, if you asked Harriet, had no more

rights than the peasants. If as many.

"Make a note of this, please," said Miss Beadle. "1381. Dates are important."

Harriet picked up her pen.

"1381," she wrote. "Peasants revolted."

"Harriet Johnson!" barked Miss Beadle. "Is that a ball point I see you using?"

Several other people who were using ball points hurried to hide them. Miss Beadle had decreed only last week that "Everyone must equip themselves with a proper pen. I will not tolerate sloppy handwriting."

When Miss Beadle said a 'proper pen', she meant one of the old-fashioned kind that used real ink. Harriet had meant to tell her mum, but she had forgotten all about it. There were so many interesting things to do at a weekend that Miss Beadle and her proper pens had quite slid from her memory.

Mrs Middleton had never insisted on proper pens. Everybody had liked Mrs Middleton: everybody hated Miss Beadle. She was only here for a term, while Mrs Middleton was away having a baby, but a term went on for ever and by the time Mrs Middleton came back Harriet would have moved to another class. If she survived that long.

"Let me see your handwriting." Miss Beadle had come storming across the classroom and was glaring over Harriet's shoulder. "As I thought! Completely unreadable!"

"I can read it," said Harriet.

"Do not be impertinent!" snapped Miss Beadle. She snatched Harriet's book away from her. "Tomorrow you will come with a proper pen and you will stay in at second break and rewrite everything that you have written today."

Harriet's freckly face turned crimson. Alison Leary, who was every teacher's pet, screwed the top back on her proper pen and sat forward with an air of eager anticipation.

"Hands up," said Miss Beadle, "anyone else who is using a ball point!"

There was a pause, then Gerry Mander's hand went up, and Stinky Allport's; and then three others in quick succession, Wendy Williams, Hake-face Heneghan and Salim Khan, pop pop pop, from different corners of the room.

Miss Beadle breathed, deeply. Her nostrils flared, her lips tightened. She strode from one side of the class to the other.

Stinky and Hake-face rolled their eyes. Gerry Mander looked scared. Wendy Williams chewed a plait.

Alison Leary sat back on her chair and smiled.

"Very well," said Miss Beadle. "If you choose to ignore my instructions you must pay the price." Her voice rose to a shriek. "I WILL NOT TOLERATE DISOBEDIENCE! Do I make myself clear?"

The class nodded.

"You will all six of you stay in with Harriet Johnson. And anyone coming to school without a proper pen will be sent straight back home again. You have been warned!"

The six culprits gathered miserably together in the playground at break.

"She can't do that!" wailed Gerry. "She's not allowed!"

"Doesn't matter whether they're allowed or not," said Harriet. "It's like lords of the manor and peasants … they just do whatever they want 'cos they've got the power and we're helpless."

"But it's not fair!"

"Wasn't fair in middle-age times. That's why they revolted."

"At least in middle-age times they weren't expected to keep on writing with proper pens all the time."

"No, 'cos they didn't write in those days. Not ordinary people didn't."

"I wouldn't mind not writing." Hake-face sounded wistful. "I don't know why we need writing, anyway. Seems to me they got on all right without it when they were peasants."

"Things were different then," said Harriet.

"No school," said Wendy.

They sighed.

"I wouldn't have minded being a peasant," said Hake-face. "Seems to me I don't know what they were complaining of."

"'Cause the lords of the manor kept stealing their best beasts." Harriet had actually been listening quite hard to the morning's lesson.

"Every time a peasant died the lord of the manor said, 'Give me your best beast.' And they all had to grind their corn at his mill and he made them pay him money for it. And whenever they got married he made them pay him more money."

"Bet he didn't make 'em buy proper pens and write down dates all the time!"

"My mum'll go mad," said Salim, "if I ask her for another pen. She already bought me one."

"So what happened to it?" said Harriet, side-tracked.

"I swopped it with someone for a share in a computer game.

"Know what I vote?" said Harriet. They looked at her. "I vote we tell her."

"Tell her what?" said Wendy.

"Tell her that we don't see why we should be forced to use proper pens when ball points are just as good and we're sick of being pushed around like peasants and not having any rights. That's what I vote."

There was a silence.

"*Well?*" said Harriet.

"Thing is," said Wendy, nervously, "it's not as if we're going to get married or anything."

Harriet rounded on her.

"What's that got to do with it?"

"What you said – people having to pay money when they got married."

"And having their best beasts took off them.

We haven't got any beasts" said Hake-face.

"I have," said Harriet. "I've got a cat."

"Me, too!" said Wendy, suddenly sounding worried.

"We've got beasts," said Harriet.

At this, some of the others remembered that they too had beasts. Stinky Allport had a stick insect, Gerry Mander had a slug, even Hake-face had a bowl of goldfish.

"I don't want her taking my goldfish!"

"Well, she will," said Harriet, "the way she's carrying on. Won't be any stopping her. What we ought to do, we ought to gather in a rout, like the peasants, and resist with strong hand."

"But her hands are stronger than ours." moaned Wendy.

"Not if we put all ours together, they're not."

"What's a rout," said Hake-face, "anyway?"

Harriet wasn't quite sure about this, but not being one for admitting to ignorance she had her answer pat: "Something you gather in, dummy!"

"Like material?" said Gerry, whose mother was a dressmaker.

"No!" howled Harriet. "Not like material."

"Like corn," said Hake-face. He opened his mouth and began droning: "All the corn is gathered in..."

"What about boils?" said Salim. "They gather."

"Not like boils!" Harriet said it angrily. She wondered if Wat Tyler had had this problem with his lot. "More like a – a circle. That's what it was! They gathered in circles and got angry and plotted. Everyone get into a circle!"

Mumbling, they did so.

"Now all move closer," instructed Harriet, "so's nobody can hear what we're plotting."

The circle moved closer.

"Now get angry!"

The circle hesitated.

"Well, go on!" screamed Harriet. "Think of all the things she's going to do to you ... keeping you in, sending you home, stealing your goldfish!"

The circle sprang to life. There was a muttering and a stumping and a vague hint of threat. Other people, attracted by this new game, came running over to join them.

Soon the whole of their class, except for Alison Leary and her best friend Snobby Clark, were in the throes of rebellion. Only a few knew what it was about, but all were agreed that action was called for.

"We've got to make a charter!" yelled Harriet. "We've got to make demands! Proper pens OUT, ball points IN!"

They took up the chant: "Proper pens OUT, ball points IN!"

"What we've got to do," said Harriet, "is have a revolt."

"Hooray!" cried Hake-face, jumping up and punching the air. "Gonna have a revolt!"

They decided that they would have the revolt next day during the lunch break.

"We'll present our demands," said Harriet, "like the peasants did to Richard II, and then they'll give us a charter saying we can use what sort of pens we like and that way she won't be able to keep us in the afternoon writing things."

"How do we have the revolt?" Salim wanted to know. "In a circle?"

"No! In a mob. We've got to be a rabble. That means making a noise," explained Harriet, "and drawing attention to our cause. Everybody bring something that makes a noise!"

After tea that day Harriet said to her mum, "Can I borrow two saucepan lids for school tomorrow?"

"Of course," said her mum, pleased. It wasn't very often that Harriet took an interest in domestic affairs. "What about the saucepans to go with them? Don't you want them as well?"

"Not really," said Harriet. "Just the lids will do. We're having a peasants' revolt and I'm Wat Tyler."

"How nice," said her mum. "Are you going to do it in public?"

Harriet frowned. "In the playground."

"Oh, I see," said her mum. "A sort of living history lesson."

"Something like that," said Harriet.

Next morning, Miss Beadle reminded them about their proper pens.

"I trust you all have them. I shall expect to see the six of you in this afternoon's break."

The six exchanged glances. Alison Leary and Snobby Clark, who didn't know what was going on, gave little titters.

During the morning, Miss Beadle shouted at Hake-face for scuffling his feet, yelled at Wendy for talking when she shouldn't have been, sent Salim to stand by the stationery cupboard, and icily informed Harriet that, "if you are not able to sit without pulling faces you had better go and report yourself to the office."

Miss Beadle deserved to be revolted against, thought Harriet, as she trundled off to the office (for the seventh time that term).

"Dear me!" said Mrs Atkins. "You again, Harriet? You do seem to be a bit of a troublemaker."

All the best people in history had been troublemakers. Boadicea, William the

Conqueror, Wat Tyler ... Harriet Johnson. You couldn't take tyranny lying down, thought Harriet.

After lunch, in the playground, they began the revolt. Harriet marched at their head, clashing her saucepan lids, with Hake-face (on the tin tray) and Stinky Allport (on the trumpet) at her side. Close behind, all bunched up as befitted a rabble, came the rest of the class. Some had brought whistles, some had brought rattles, Kevin Potter had an old car horn, Tracey Biggins had a dog's squeaky toy. Salim had a megaphone, through which he chanted as he marched : "Proper pens OUT, ball points IN! Proper pens OUT, ball points IN!"

People started rallying from all corners of the playground. Before very long, a whole gaggle of children from other classes were marching along with the revolt, joyously taking up the chant: "Proper pens OUT, ball points IN!"

Wendy Williams waved a length of stick with a piece of card stuck on to it. On the card were the words, **HANDS OFF OUR BEASTS**! The word spread like wildfire through the serried ranks of marchers: Miss Beadle was going to steal all their best hamsters and gerbils and goldfish!

The revolt grew apace. Round the playground they marched, whistles blowing, hooters hooting, saucepan lids clashing. Only Alison Leary and her friend Snobby Clark remained aloof.

"They'll be for it," said Alison. "You just wait till Miss Beadle sees them!"

The bell had rung for the start of afternoon school, but no one save Alison and Snobby heard it. These two stuck their noses in the air and smiled superior smiles as they strolled off, arm in arm, across the playground.

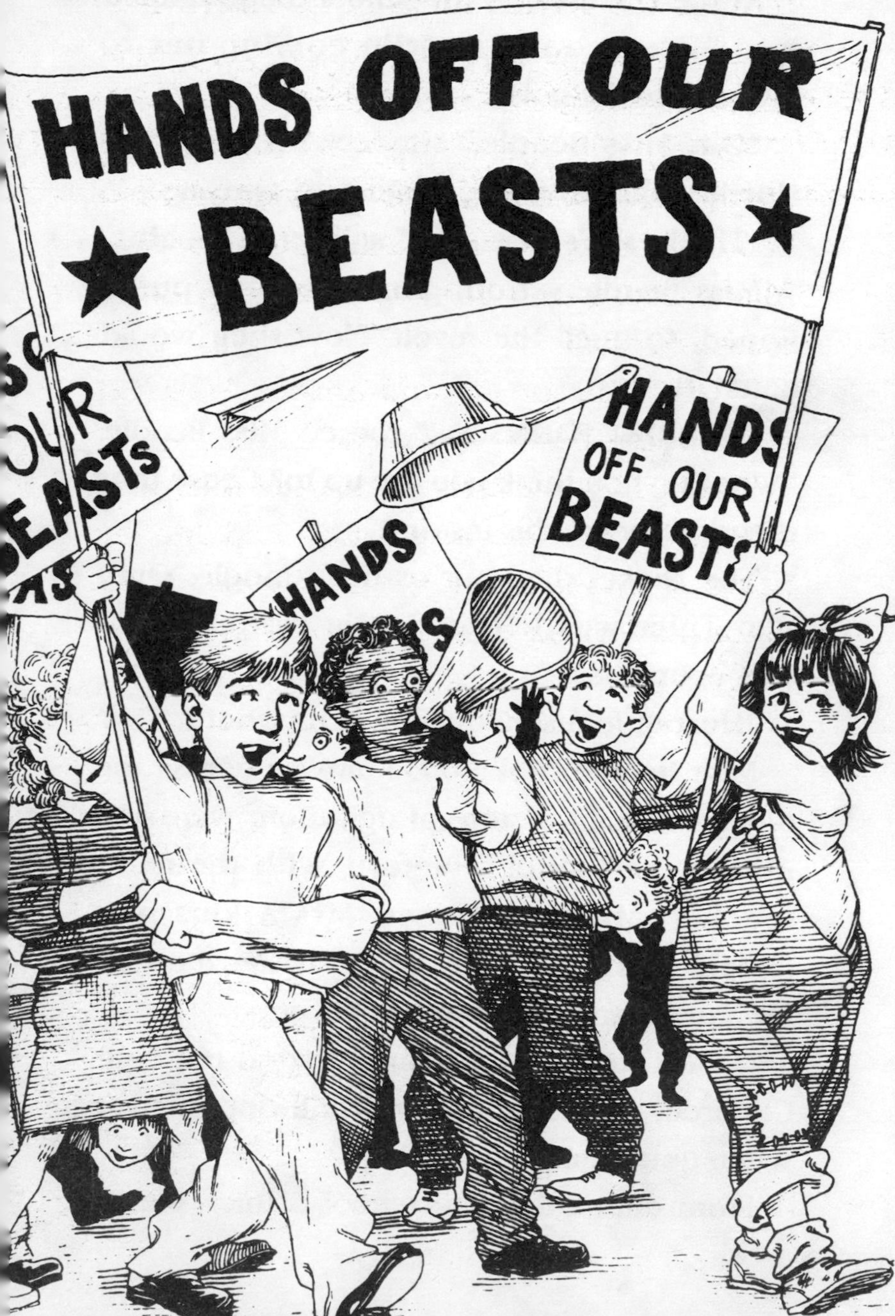
HANDS OFF OUR BEASTS
OUR BEASTS
HANDS
HANDS OFF OUR BEASTS

At the entrance to the school they bumped into Miss Beadle, angrily coming out to investigate the noise.

"Oh, Miss Beadle," simpered Alison, "It's Harriet Johnson trying to start an uprising."

"Thinks she's Wat Tyler," sniggered Snobby.

Miss Beadle set off, grim-faced and purse-lipped, to quell the revolt. Now they would catch it!

"HARRIET JOHNSON!" roared Miss Beadle. "What do you think you are up to? Cease that dreadful racket this instant!"

The racket died out as if by magic. Only Wat Tyler was left, defiantly clattering his saucepan lids.

"Harriet Johnson, did you hear what I..."

Miss Beadle broke off. Running across the playground, in a state of agitation, were Mrs Atkins, the school secretary, with the head teacher, Mr Marsh-Jones. Mrs Atkins was clutching a stack of registers to her bosom, Mr Marsh-Jones was waving his arms.

"Quick, quick, Mrs Atkins! Take a roll call! Children, please stand quite still and answer when your names are called."

From one end of the school a thick plume

of smoke could be seen rising. The school was on fire!

Miss Beadle screamed.

"Alison Leary and Jennifer Clark!"

"You think they started it?" said Mr Marsh-Jones.

"No, no! They're in the building!"

At that moment, Alison and Snobby appeared, looking pale and frightened, led out by one of the teachers. The rest of the teachers stumbled after them, coughing and spluttering, their handkerchiefs held to their noses.

Everybody else, every single child, was already out there, in the playground, participating in the revolt.

"Thank heavens for that!" cried Mr Marsh-Jones.

"Children, a terrible thing has happened ... our lovely new fire alarm failed to go off. Fortunately no harm has been done, apart from the classrooms being filled with smoke, but I'm afraid we shall all have to stay out here in the playground until it's time to go home."

At this, great rejoicings broke out among

the ranks of the revolt. No break time detention! No staying in to write with proper pens! Fun and games in the playground!

"I have to say," said Mr Marsh-Jones, "that had it not been for some very quick thinking on the part of Harriet Johnson –" he beamed upon Harriet, as she stood there with her saucepan lids, "– the situation might well have been disastrous. As it was, she called you all here and kept you at her side. Well done, Harriet!"

Harriet tried not to smirk, though it was difficult with Alison and Snobby standing there twitching.

"I don't know what you thought you were up to," hissed Miss Beadle. (Not having so nice a nature, she was not as easily fooled as Mr Marsh-Jones.) "But whatever it was –" Harriet raised her eyes, innocently "– I think I should warn you that the leaders of uprisings almost always come to sticky ends. Wat Tyler, for instance, was slain at Smithfield in the presence of his mob. I tell you this," hissed Miss Beadle, " for your own good."

"Three cheers for Harriet!" cried Mr Marsh-Jones. "Hip, hip…"

"Hooray!" cried everyone except Alison Leary, Snobby Clark and Miss Beadle.

"Well! That was a pretty good revolt," said Hake-face, as the rabble broke up and went about its business. "I reckon we ought to have another one some day."

"You can be Wat Tyler next time," said Harriet.

She didn't believe in pushing her luck.

THE BEAUTIFUL BABY
COMPETITION

There was great excitement in the Johnson family: Auntie Margaret had come over from America with her new baby.

Dad was excited because Auntie Margaret was his sister and they hadn't seen each other for almost two years. Mum was excited because she was now an aunt. Lynn was excited because she was a cousin. They were also excited about seeing the baby.

Harriet, on the other hand, couldn't have cared less about the baby. Harriet was excited because Auntie Margaret had brought her a real proper baseball cap with NEW YORK YANKEES written on it. To Harriet's way of thinking, a baseball cap was far more exciting than a baby. Harriet didn't go for babies; nasty smelly things if you asked her.

She thought it absolutely pathetic the way

the family all crooned over it.

"Who's a lovely boy, then?" said Dad, waggling his fingers.

"Bless him!" said Mum, with a soppy smile.

"He's really cute," said Lynn, jiggling him up and down on her lap.

Sickening!

"Would you like to hold him, Harriet?" said Auntie Margaret.

Fortunately, because Harriet wouldn't have wanted to hurt Auntie Margaret's feelings by saying no, her mum leapt in with a screech of horror.

"Don't let Harriet anywhere near him! She'd only drop him!"

"I would not!" Harriet said it indignantly. She didn't drop Fat Cat; why should she drop the baby? She bet Fat Cat was at least twice as heavy.

She was glad, all the same, when the thing was put back in its carry cot. You never knew with babies. They might suddenly decide to throw up all over you or do things in their nappies. Horrible!

Harriet left the family to coo and gurgle while she stuck her baseball cap on her head and swaggered up to the park to see who was there. She found Wendy Williams, idly swinging on a swing, and Stinky Allport and Salim Khan half-heartedly attempting to climb a tree.

"Look what I've got!" said Harriet, brandishing her cap.

They looked.

"Let's have a go of it," said Stinky.

The baseball cap was duly passed round and admired. Everyone agreed that it was brilliant, but really and truly, once you'd tried it on, both back-to-front and the right way round, there wasn't very much else that you could do with it.

Wendy sighed.

"It gets kind of boring," she said, "just sitting here."

"Why don't we do something?" said Harriet.

"Do what?" said Salim.

"I don't know! Anything!"

"We've tried it," said Stinky.

They'd tried kicking a ball, they'd tried tracking, they'd tried throwing stones at Coca Cola cans. They'd tried climbing on the roof of the sports pavilion and been bawled at by the park keeper.

They'd tried lobbing sticks into the infant's paddling pool and been bawled at by an outraged mother. They'd tried just about everything they could think of.

"I'm bored," said Wendy.

"Me too," said Salim.

"But you can't be!" wailed Harriet. "It's half term!"

Another four days stretched emptily before then.

"Haven't got any money," said Stinky, "that's what it is."

Harriet hadn't got any money, either. If she

had had money, she could have bought a baseball bat to go with her cap and they could have practised baseball.

Harriet sank down moodily on the swing next to Wendy.

"My aunt's come over from America and brought her baby," she said.

"Ugh! Yuck!" said Wendy.

Stinky made a being-sick noise.

"I know," said Harriet. "It's *gruesome*."

Salim sat on the swing next to Harriet's and launched himself into the air.

"I like babies," he said.

They studied him a while as if he were some peculiar kind of bug that had crawled out of a hole.

"You're batty," said Harriet. "They don't do anything except just cry and make messes. They're *useless*."

They weren't only useless, they took over the entire household. Nobody had eyes for anything except the baby. It only had to open its mouth and squeak and they all went running.

"I suppose you're jealous," said Lynn to Harriet.

"No, I'm not," said Harriet.

She wasn't in the least bit jealous; she just couldn't see what all the fuss was about.

That evening, over tea, they talked non-stop about the baby.

"He's going to look just like his dad!" said Harriet's mum.

"Spitting image," said Harriet's dad.

"I wish I'd got a baby brother," said Lynn.

Faintly, as if from a distance, Harriet heard Auntie Margaret say, "Did I tell you I entered him for a beautiful baby competition and he got first prize?"

Coos and gurgles. Delighted cries of, "What a clever little man! Oh, *isn't* he a clever little man!"

Harriet looked up, frowning.

"What was the prize?" she said.

Auntie Margaret proudly informed her, "An engraved silver cup and fifty dollars."

"Fifty *dollars*?" said Harriet.

"Well – you know! It was just a token gesture."

Fifty dollars didn't sound like a token gesture to Harriet: fifty dollars sounded like serious money. Sternly she turned her attention to the baby, sitting on its mother's lap, dribbling.

Its face was smeared in a revolting mess of mashed banana. It didn't look much like a beautiful baby to Harriet. It was all gummy and hairless with a strange blobby nose.

"How much is fifty dollars in English money?" said Harriet.

"Oh... about thirty-five pounds, I would say."

Thirty-five pounds! That would buy a baseball bat for sure.

"Where did they get the money from?" she said.

"Why, everybody who entered the competition had to pay an entrance fee. I guess they took it out of that."

"And then they got to keep the rest themselves?"

"I suppose they would have kept some of it. Just enough to cover their costs."

Harriet couldn't wait to get to the park next morning.

"I've had an idea!" announced Harriet. "An idea for making money!"

All they had to do was hold a beautiful baby competition of their own. They could write out notices, and tell all their friends, and everyone would pay an entrance fee and the winner would get a prize and whatever was left over would buy a baseball bat so that they could practise baseball and stop being bored.

"What do you think of *that*?" said Harriet.

There was a pause.

"Where would we get the babies from?" said Stinky.

"*We* wouldn't have to get the babies. Other people would get the babies – the ones that entered the competition."

"Can I enter it?" said Salim. "I could enter my baby sister."

Wendy brightened. "My brother's got a baby. I could enter him!"

"You'd have to pay the entrance fee," said Harriet.

"How much would it be?"

"Mm … fifty pence?"

"And how much would I win if I won?"

"Depends on how much we make."

"You'd have to say," said Wendy. "Nobody'll bother entering unless you say."

"All right, then. First Prize…" Harriet did a quick sum in her head; she was good at mental arithmetic. "First prize, five pounds."

That way, if fifty people entered – and it was difficult to imagine *fewer* than fifty people entering – they would be left with twenty pounds to spend on a baseball bat.

"What about second prize?"

"Can't afford a second prize."

"There's always a second prize," said Wendy. "*Always.*"

After some discussion they decided that the second prize should be a certificate. Salim would write it out, because he had the best handwriting, and Wendy would decorate it with pretty curves and squiggles so that whoever won it could hang it on the wall.

"What about the cup?" Salim wanted to know.

"What cup?"

"You said your aunt's baby got a silver cup – an *engraved* silver cup."

"We could give 'em a mug," said Stinky. "My mum's got lots of old mugs. I could get one of those and paint things on it."

"And where're we going to hold it?" said Wendy.

"In the park."

"Suppose it rains?"

Harriet looked at Wendy, crossly. Why was it that some people could think of nothing better to do than raise objections?

"The shelter!" said Salim. "We could hold it in the shelter!"

"That's what I meant," said Harriet, who hadn't meant anything of the kind. She had forgotten about the shelter. It was hidden away in a corner of the park and was a bit dilapidated, but at least it had a roof on it.

The shelter would do perfectly!

They parted company, Stinky to paint things on one of his mother's old mugs, Salim to write out the certificate in his best handwriting, Wendy to decorate it with pretty squiggles and Harriet to type out a notice on her mum's word processor.

Harriet's notice read:

BEAUTIFUL BABY COMPETITION

to be held in
THE SHELTER IN THE PARK
tomorrow morning at 11 o'clock
First Prize: £5 and a mug
Second prize: A decorated certificate
To enter come to the Shelter **NOW**
(Bring your 50p with you)

"I put that bit in," she explained, as the four of them met up again after lunch, "in case anyone thinks they can get away without paying."

"Better hadn't!" said Stinky.

Harriet had printed ten copies of her leaflet. They stuck them with sticky tape all

over the park; then they retired to the shelter to await results.

By the end of the afternoon, eighteen people had made their way to the shelter and paid their fifty pences. Most of them were people that they knew from school, or from seeing in the park. There weren't any grown-ups, but then they hadn't expected that.

Harriet took the money home with her for safe keeping. Eighteen times fifty pence was nine pounds, and five pounds of *that* was prize money. That only left four pounds.

Four pounds wasn't anywhere near enough! Harriet racked her brains for a way to make more.

Suppose *she* found a baby that she could enter? That would mean there were three of them, her and Wendy and Salim, who all stood a chance of winning; and if any of them were lucky, then naturally the prize money would go towards buying the baseball bat.

Harriet wondered where she could get a baby from. There was absolutely no point in asking Auntie Margaret for hers; Auntie Margaret knew Harriet too well. She knew that Harriet was prone to unfortunate accidents. It would be just like Harriet to put the baby down somewhere and forget where she had put it, or even to put it down somewhere and forget she'd ever had it. She wouldn't, of course, but that was what Auntie Margaret would *say*.

Where was there a baby whose mother wasn't prejudiced against her?

Harriet thought about it. There was the new lady next door. The new lady had moved in about six weeks ago, which would normally be quite long enough for someone to get to know Harriet – everyone in the road knew Harriet – but the lady next door had broken her leg the very week that she had moved and had had to go into hospital to have it mended.

She had only been home a few days and was still walking with a limp. She would probably be only too happy for Harriet to borrow her baby.

Immediately after breakfast next morning, Harriet went round to see her.

"Good morning," said Harriet. "I'm Harriet, I live next door."

She waited for the lady to scream or turn pale (which was what people quite often did when Harriet came to call on them) but the lady only smiled and said, "How nice to meet you, Harriet! I'm Mrs Wade. What can I do for you?"

Harriet beamed.

"I was wondering," said Harriet, "if you'd like me to take your baby up to the park … some of my friends are taking their baby brothers and sisters up there. I thought perhaps it would be nice for it. Seeing as you can't walk very far."

"What a kind thought!" said Mrs. Wade. "I'm sure she'd love to meet some other babies. That's very sweet of you, Harriet."

"So when shall I take her?" said Harriet. "Shall I call round at about quarter to eleven?"

"Why not? I'll make sure she's ready for you."

Promptly at quarter to eleven, Harriet called to collect her baby. Its name, said Mrs Wade, was Cordelia, though it might just as well have been Emma or Tracey since it didn't show any signs of recognising it. Imagine not knowing its own name! Even Fat Cat knew that he was called Fat Cat. Still, it wasn't a bad sort of baby as babies went. It smiled quite nicely and blew bubbles; it might stand a chance of winning.

Proudly, Harriet pushed her push chair up to the park. A great gaggle of children and babies were already there, crammed together in the shelter. Stinky explained excitedly to Harriet that he had collected another three pounds fifty in entrance fees.

"And that's not counting Wendy and Salim."

"Or me," said Harriet. She waved a careless hand at her push chair. "I've brought this one along ... it doesn't know its name but it's quite pretty."

A belligerent-looking girl with red hair came up and demanded to know when the competition was going to begin.

"Soon," said Harriet, who didn't intend letting anyone boss her around. This was her show: she would say when it began.

"It better had be soon," said the girl. "I can't hang about all morning, I'm only s'pposed to have just taken it just up the road."

Other people began saying that they, too, were only supposed to have taken theirs just up the road.

"If we don't start soon, you can give me my money back."

"All right, all right! We'll start immediately," said Harriet. "But we've got to have more room"

The shelter was so crowded, you could hardly see the babies for the people who had brought them. Also, some of the babies had started screaming, and some of the babies had started wailing, and all the rest of the babies looked as if they were about to start doing one or the other at any moment, and how were you supposed to judge which was the most beautiful when your eardrums were being shattered?

"Get all the babies out of their buggies and put them on the floor," commanded Harriet. "Then get all the buggies outside so's we have room to move."

The girl with red hair said she wasn't putting her one on the floor. "It might be dirty."

"So put it on a coat or something!" shrieked Harriet. After a certain amount of mumbling and muttering, and a lot of screaming and wailing, all the push chairs were outside and all the babies were inside, crawling about the floor on an assortment of clothes.

"That's better," said Harriet. "Now you lot go and stand over there and we'll do the judging."

"Hang about!" It was the girl with red hair again. She was obviously one of those who like to make a nuisance of themselves. "How can you do the judging when one of them's yours?"

Harriet hadn't thought about that. For a moment she was at a loss; but Harriet was not a girl who was ever at a loss for very long.

"He can do it." She jerked a thumb at Stinky. "He's not got one."

"No, but you're all in it together," said the girl. "You and him and them two. He'll just go and choose one of yours."

"I won't" said Stinky. "I don't know which their ones are."

"You know which one his is," said the girl, witheringly. She nodded at Salim's baby sister.

"Well, I won't choose her, then," said Stinky.

Salim then said heatedly that that wasn't fair, he'd paid his fifty pence the same as anyone else. The red-haired girl agreed.

"Seems to me *none* of it's fair. It's nothing but a con!"

Quickly, before she could have a revolution on her hands, Harriet made a decision.

"I'll go and look in the park and find someone else to do the judging."

"Yeah, an' I'll come with you an' all." said the girl with red hair.

Harriet and Red-head left the shelter together.

"We'll ask the first person we see," said Harriet.

The first person they saw was a teenage girl eating a bag of crisps.

"D'you want to come and judge a beautiful baby competition?" said Harriet.

"Not particularly." said the girl.

"I'll give you fifty pence," said Harriet.

"All right." The girl screwed up her crisp bag. "Where are they?"

Harriet and Red-head led her across to the shelter.

"There," said Harriet.

The girl studied them, critically.

"They all look the same to me," she said.

"Just get on and choose one!" hissed Red-head. "I got to get home before my mum starts wondering where I am."

"OK." The girl pointed. "That one."

"Which one?" said Harriet.

"That one in yellow. Where's my fifty pence?"

Harriet handed it over. Red-head, disgusted, snatched up one of the babies and stalked off. Other people, equally disgusted, followed suit. Nobody seemed interested in knowing who had won the second prize. In the end, there were only two babies left, the one in yellow who had been judged most beautiful, and one in white, or what had started off as white; it was now more of a sort of dirty grey.

Harriet looked across at Wendy. Everyone else, except for Stinky and Salim, who had strapped his baby sister back in her push chair, had gone.

"Which one's yours?" said Harriet.

"That one," said Wendy. "I think." She pointed rather dubiously at the prize winner.

"OK." said Harriet. She could afford to be generous. So long as one of them had won, that was all that mattered. As an afterthought she added, "Mine's called Cordelia. What's yours?"

"Fred." said Wendy.

"Try talking to it and see what happens."

"Fred?" said Wendy. The baby in yellow smiled a big gappy smile. Harriet nodded.

"Right. You take the mug. I'll hang on to the five pounds. After lunch we'll go look at baseball bats."

Harriet settled her baby in its push chair and raced triumphantly back with it to Mrs Wade.

"There you are," she said. "She's been in the park and met lots of other babies and…"

Mrs Wade screamed, loudly.

"That's not Cordelia!"

"What?" said Harriet.

"That's not Cordelia! That's not my baby! Oh, my God, what have you done with her?"

"I haven't done anything with her," said Harriet. "I just took her up to the park and..."

With a howl, Mrs Wade grabbed the push chair in one hand, Harriet in the other, and dragged them both round to Harriet's house.

"What on earth...?" began Harriet's mum. She looked grimly from Mrs Wade to the baby to Harriet. "I think you'd better come in," she said.

In the front room were the red-haired girl, with a red-haired woman and a spindly baby in a push chair.

"Angelica!" cried the red-haired woman, making a dive for Harriet's baby.

"What have you done with my Cordelia?" wept Mrs Wade.

At that moment, there was a ring at the front door. Harriet's mum went to answer it. She returned with Wendy, holding the prize-winning mug, and Wendy's mum, holding a big pink baby dressed in yellow.

"Cordelia!" cried Mrs Wade, leaping forward.

"Fred!" cried Wendy's mum, snatching up the spindly baby.

Harriet's mum turned to Harriet.

"Might I suggest," said Harriet's mum, in icy tones, "that you tell us what has been going on?"

"I can explain!" said Harriet.

She did so, at some length. In fact she went on for so long that by the time she came to the end only her mum and Mrs Wade were left to hear it.

" – and there wasn't any room so we took them out their buggies and put them on the floor – well, not on the floor exactly. On coats and stuff so's they wouldn't get dirty. And then – "

"Just stop talking, Harriet!" Her mum clapped both hands to her ears. "We've heard enough!"

"But I haven't got to the best bit yet! The best bit," said Harriet, "is that my baby – I mean Mrs Wade's baby – I mean, *Cordelia*, has won the first prize! She's won the cup. Look!" Harriet held out Stinky's mum's old mug, round the rim of which, in wobbly red letters, Stinky had written the words, **MOST BEAUTY FULL BABY**.

"Isn't is lovely?" said Harriet.

There was a pause. Harriet's mum looked

nervously at Mrs Wade. Mrs Wade looked at the mug – and Cordelia stretched out her hands.

"She wants it!" said Harriet, enchanted. "She wants her mug!"

Cordelia was not only a beautiful baby, she was obviously a highly intelligent baby (in spite of answering to the name of Fred).

"There you are," said Harriet.

Everyone looked at Cordelia, cuddling her mug. A fond maternal smile crossed Mrs Wade's features.

"I suppose in the circumstances," she said, "no real harm has been done."

"Even so – " Harriet's mum turned sternly on her, as the front door closed behind the prize-winning baby and its proud mother – "straight after lunch, my girl, you can sit yourself down and write some letters of apology!"

And after that, thought Harriet, jingling the coins in her jeans pocket, she would go and collect the others from the park and they would all go down the road to buy their baseball bat...